MOST LOVED MONSTER

by Lynn Downey — illustrations by Jack E. Davis

Dial Books for Young Readers ☩ New York

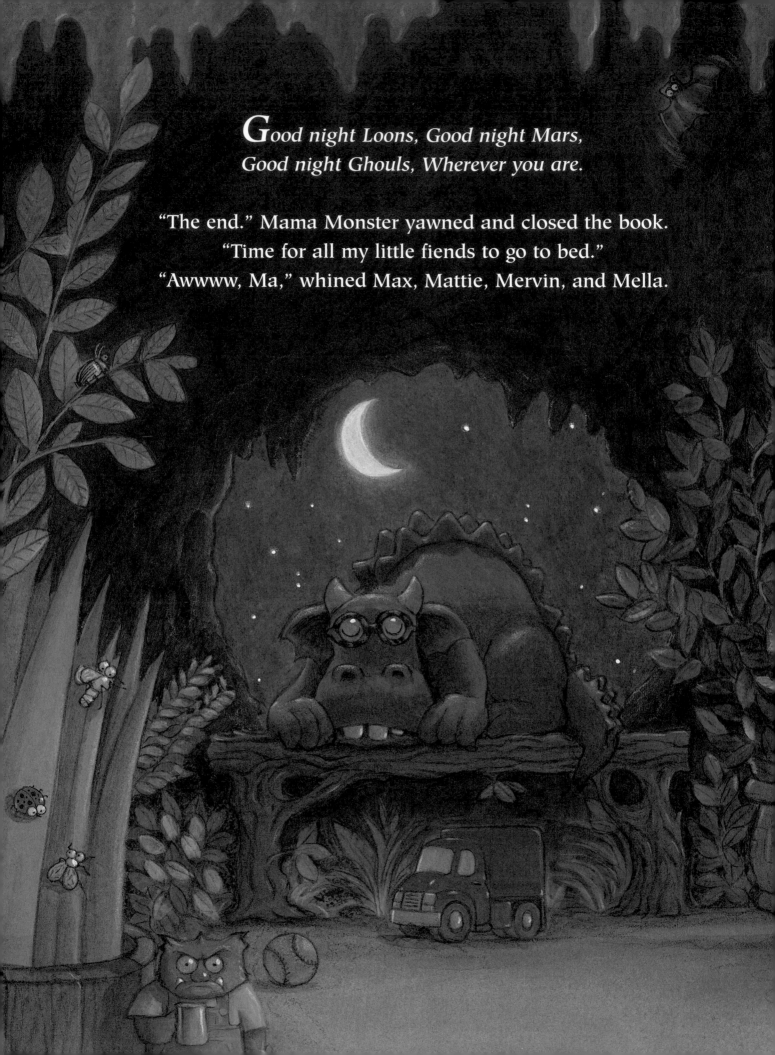

*G*ood night Loons, Good night Mars,
Good night Ghouls, Wherever you are.

"The end." Mama Monster yawned and closed the book.
"Time for all my little fiends to go to bed."
"Awwww, Ma," whined Max, Mattie, Mervin, and Mella.

"Don't forget to brush your fangs and floss," she added.
"And remove all ticks and moss."

After they'd washed and brushed and crept into their beds,
Mama tippy-clawed into Max's room.

"Good night, my love," Mama said.

"Mama?" shrieked Max. "Who do you love most?"

"I love *all* my little monsters. But you—you are very special."

Max shrugged. "Me? What makes me so special?"

"You have a wonderful sense of humor." Mama smiled.
"You tell the funniest bang-bang jokes. And I love it when
you twist your horns and make your eyeballs pop out."

Max grinned. "I *am* funny, aren't I?"

"You are my beast. Now get some rest. It's time for dreams."

And Max closed his eyes with a smile in his heart
as Mama crept into Mattie's room.

"Good night, my love," Mama said.

"Mama?" croaked Mattie. "Who do you love most?"

"I love *all* my little monsters. But you—you are very special."

Mattie shrugged. "How? How am I so special?"

"You have the nicest manners." Mama smiled.
"You always scream out in school and you never raise
your hand. You share your spit, and you're *always*
lugging old monsters across the street."

Mattie grinned. "I *am* polite, aren't I?"

"You are my beast. Now get some rest. It's time for dreams."

And Mattie closed her eyes with a smile in her heart
as Mama crept into Mervin's room.

"Good night, my love," Mama said.

"Mama?" hissed Mervin. "Who do you love most?"

"I love *all* my little monsters. But you—you are very special."

Mervin shrugged. "Why? Why am I so special?"

"You're so creative." Mama smiled.
"The way you color all over the walls and sculpt
dragons in your mossed potatoes. And your
Dragonfly Pie is the slimiest I've ever tasted!"

Mervin grinned. "I *am* creative, aren't I?"

"You are my beast. Now get some rest. It's time for dreams."

And Mervin closed his eyes with a smile in his heart
as Mama crept into Mella's room.

"Good night, my love," Mama said.

"Mama?" growled Mella. "Who do you love most?"

"I love *all* my little monsters. But you—you are very special."

Mella shrugged. "Me? Why me?"

"You're so brave." Mama smiled.
"You stand up to the biggest bullies at the play pond and you're
always rescuing smaller monsters from the Fierce Dragonflies—
and you're *never* afraid to dive into the deep end of the tar pit."

Mella grinned. "I *am* brave, aren't I?"

"You are my beast. Now get some rest. It's time for dreams."

And Mella closed her eyes with a smile in her heart
as Mama crept out of the room.

When Mama reached her bed, she fell fast asleep. As her snores rattled the walls, she didn't hear the tippy-claw, tippy-claw of four little beasts, cackling as they scampered about the cave.

Mervin baked his most creative recipe yet—roachberry upside-down cake with mud-covered slugs on top.

Mattie *hukkkked* hairballs and
wrapped them in stinkweed.

Mella set her gooiest tar pit bone on Mama's favorite chair.

And Max came up with his best joke ever:

Bang-bang.
Who's there?
Fang.
Fang who?
Fang you for loving me!

Early the next morning, Mama tippy-clawed downstairs while
her little monsters listened quietly from their beds.

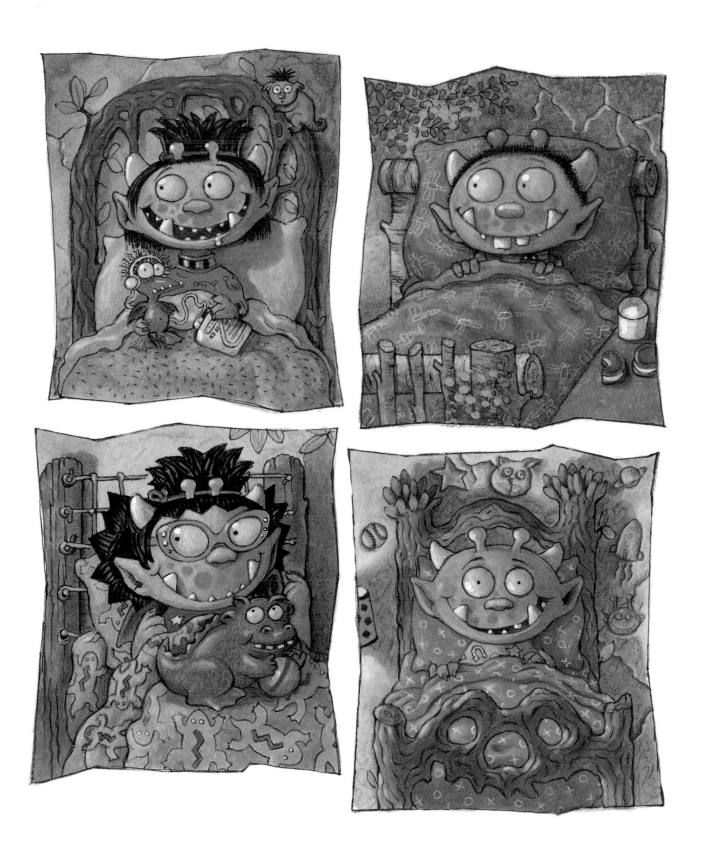

And as they heard her howl with happiness, all the little
monsters giggled and thought: I *knew* she loved me most!

"Oh, Max!" Mama exclaimed. "Oh, Mattie, Mervin, and Mella! You are *all* so very special!"

Then she turned around and there smeared across the cave walls were the words:

To my three little monsters with love
—L.D.

For Betty and Marie
—J.E.D.

Published by Dial Books for Young Readers
A division of Penguin Young Readers Group
345 Hudson Street, New York, New York 10014
Text copyright © 2004 by Lynn Downey
Pictures copyright © 2004 by Jack E. Davis
All rights reserved
Designed by Lily Malcom
Text set in Hiroshige Medium
Manufactured in China on acid-free paper
1 3 5 7 9 10 8 6 4 2

Library of Congress Cataloging-in-Publication Data
Downey, Lynn, date.
Most loved monster / by Lynn Downey ;
illustrations by Jack E. Davis.
p. cm.
Summary: At bedtime, four little monsters ask their mother which one
she loves the most, and one by one, she reminds them of why they
are special. Later, they return the compliment to their mother.
ISBN 0-8037-2728-3
[1. Mother and child—Fiction. 2. Individuality—Fiction.
3. Monsters—Fiction.] I. Davis, Jack E., ill. II. Title.
PZ7.D75915 Wh 2004
[E]—dc21
2002006821

The art was created using colored pencil, acrylic, dye, and ink.